92

The Legend of the
Orange Princess

The Legend of the
Orange Princess

retold and illustrated by

Mehlli Gobhai

HOLIDAY HOUSE, INC. • NEW YORK

In Memory of Nuru

Far from the big, bustling cities of India, in the heart of a dense jungle, stands a marble pavilion, pale as the moon. A cool, clear stream runs close by. On its banks grows a single orange tree, heavy with lustrous fruit. Few have ever passed this way, for the jungle keeps its secret well.

Some miles away lies the ruined city of Chandpur. No one lives there now except the snakes and the lizards. Yet once Chandpur was a great city, ruled by a rich and powerful king.

One bright morning, a long time ago, there was great excitement in the palace. Word was brought to the king that he had become a father.

The king rushed to the queen's chambers. When he reached her bedside he found her weeping. At first he could see nothing beside her on the bed. But when he bent down to look more closely he saw why his queen wept. She had given birth to an orange!

For a few moments the king could hardly speak. Then, very tenderly, he picked up the shining little orange and smiled at his queen.

"It is the most beautiful orange in the whole world," he whispered.

They named the little orange Narangi and decreed that she be treated as a princess.

When the royal couple sat in the pleasure pavilion, the glowing little orange was always there, resting between them on a silken cushion.

When the king held court, the ladies did not appear. Narangi sat on the queen's lap, looking down on the great hall from a screened window high above.

One evening, many years later, a young
man stopped to water his tired horse
outside the city walls. He was Prince Prithvi
of the neighboring kingdom of Boondh,
and he was a splendid sight to behold.

As he stood by the water's edge, he saw a group of young women walking toward the river. One of them carried a cushion and on it the prince thought he saw an orange.

Prince Prithvi quickly hid himself in the bushes. He saw the women carefully place the cushion under a tree and leave.

As the sun sank behind the city, the orange opened slowly and a young girl stepped forth.

The prince had never seen such a beautiful maiden. Her face had a radiance that put the full moon to shame. When she stepped into the water to bathe, her flawless body was like a flame kindling the dark river.

After a while she was joined by her handmaidens. They dried and combed her long hair and dressed her in flowing silks.

All night long they sang and danced while the spellbound prince watched.

Then as the sky grew light with the dawn, the princess slowly walked back to the orange and faded from sight.

In a daze Prince Prithvi rode back to the palace at Boondh and knelt before his royal parents.

"I am in love," said the prince, "with an orange, and I want her for my bride."

"Did you say an orange?" gasped the queen.

"What orange?" choked the king.

"She lives in the palace at Chandpur and she has stolen my mind," sighed the prince.

The poor king and queen thought that their beloved son was mad. For days the prince lay in his room not eating or drinking.

"He is bewitched," said the queen. "We must find that orange!"

And so, the king of Boondh wrote to the king of Chandpur, asking for the orange as a bride for his son.

The chief minister himself was sent to Chandpur on the royal elephant, carrying the letter on a tray of gold.

The king and queen of Chandpur were delighted to give their consent to the marriage. And so, in great pomp and splendor, Prince Prithvi of Boondh was married to Narangi, the orange princess.

Every evening, for many years, the prince retired alone to his chambers, carrying the magical orange with him.

As the sun went down, his beautiful princess was beside him again. But each morning, before the sun rose, she returned to the orange.

One evening, as the princess emerged from the orange, she found that the prince was not with her. Then she saw the prince's hunting falcon perched on the windowsill and she knew something was wrong. Taking the falcon on her wrist, she called for her horse and rode swiftly from the palace.

As soon as they were outside the city, the bird flew off, leading her deeper and deeper into the jungle.

When they were many miles from the palace, the bird began circling above Narangi's head. The princess stopped and looked around.

Lying by a small stream was the prince. Narangi rushed to his side. She felt a fever burning in his body.

Swiftly she plucked the flowers from a neem tree, crushed the petals, and poured the bitter juice through the prince's lips. All night long she cooled his body with damp leaves. Slowly the fever began to leave him.

The stars were fading and Narangi heard the clear morning song of the kokila bird. She knew that she should start for the palace to reach the orange before sunrise. But she could not leave the prince.

Slowly the sky became lighter and the
jungle was filled with the noise of the
waking birds. Prince Prithvi woke to
find his princess by his side. Then he
saw the sun creeping up through the
trees. Desperately he tried to shield
Narangi but it was too late. As the sun
came blazing over the treetops, the
orange princess vanished into the
morning air.

On the spot where she had vanished, there
now stood an orange tree, glowing and
shimmering in the sun.

Prince Prithvi had a marble pavilion
built by the stream. Every evening, for the
rest of his life, he came to the pavilion
beside the orange tree. As the sun went
down, he heard the gentle whispering of the
leaves and a soft, fragrant breeze touched
his cheek.

Then Prince Prithvi would smile, for he
knew that Narangi, his orange princess,
was beside him again.

Judith Trieste

About the Author/Artist

Mehlli Gobhai was born in Bombay, India and now lives in New York City. He makes frequent trips back to India to gather material for his books. He received his B.A. there before going to the Royal College of Art in London.

Mr. Gobhai has worked as an art director in Bombay, London and New York but now devotes much of his time to writing and illustrating children's books. He is the author/artist of five children's books, including *USHA, the Mouse Maiden,* and has also illustrated several books by other authors.